Stanley was four feet tall, about a foot wide and half an inch thick.

He had been flat ever since a bulletin board fell on him.

People in Stanley's town liked having a flat boy around.

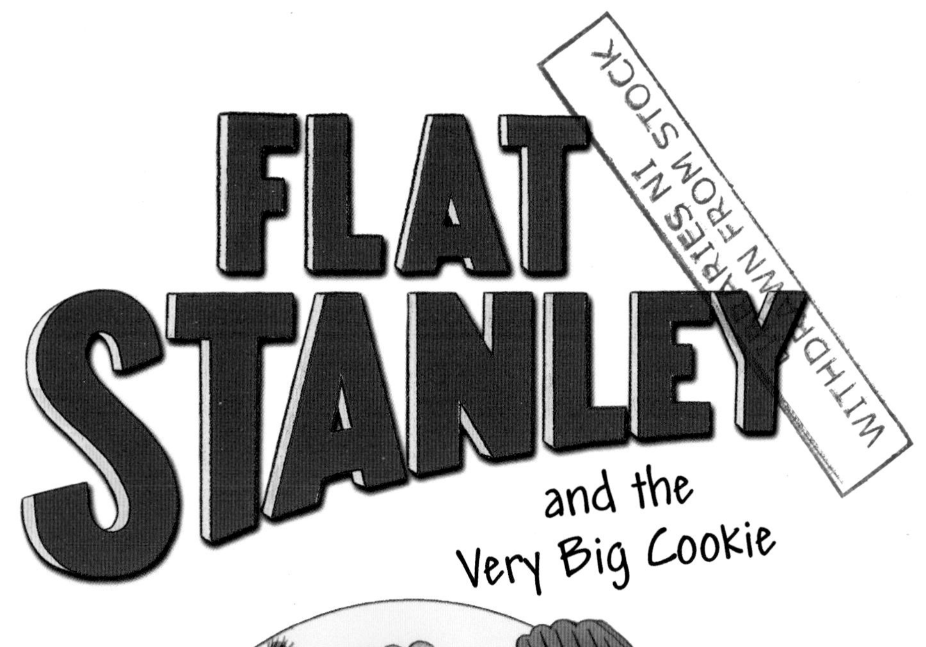

FLAT STANLEY

and the Very Big Cookie

Written by Lori Haskins Houran   Illustrations by Jon Mitchell

Based on the original character created by Jeff Brown

Reading Ladder

Stanley Lambchop lived with his mother, his father and his little brother, Arthur.

Especially since Stanley was always willing to lend a hand.

Or even a whole arm.

He helped the librarian reach books that slipped under the shelves.

S
SLIMMING

He helped the dentist smooth out the new wallpaper in his office.

And when the baker was busy, Stanley helped him ice cakes, two at a time!

But one day, Stanley and Arthur went to Pete's Sweets and found that the baker wasn't busy at all.

‘What’s wrong?’ asked Stanley.

‘It’s the baker in the next town,’ said Pete. ‘He’s taking away all my business!’

'But how?' Stanley asked. 'What does he have that you don't?'

'One word,' Pete said. 'Cupcakes.'

‘Oh, cupcakes! Yummy!’ said Arthur.

Stanley elbowed his brother.

‘What?’ Arthur said. ‘They are!’

‘It’s true,’ said Pete, looking glum.
‘They are yummy.’

‘So why don’t you bake them too?’

suggested Stanley.

‘I never copy another baker,’ said Pete. ‘I’m the one with the big ideas! The tart trend? I started that. The cherry icing craze? Me again!’

Then Pete held up a flyer.

‘This is my chance to get back my customers,’ said Pete. ‘I have to think of the next big idea by Saturday.’
He threw his hands in the air. A cloud of flour flew up.

‘If I don’t, my bakery is doomed!’

That night, Stanley and Arthur tried to think of an idea for Pete.

Mini muffins? Bite-size brownies?

Everything had been done before.

‘How about a nice coconut macaroon?’ suggested Mrs Lambchop.

The boys didn't know what a macaroon was, but it didn't sound like it could beat a cupcake.

The next day was Friday.

Stanley and Arthur stopped by the bakery after school.

It was a mess! There was icing everywhere.

One whole table was covered with cookie dough.

Candy balls were rolling around on the floor.

'Mr Pete!' called Stanley. 'What's going on? WHOA!'

Stanley slipped on a candy ball. His flat arms spun around like a windmill as he tried not to fall!

Pete came out of the kitchen just in time to see Stanley land face-first in the cookie dough! SMACK!

Arthur peeled his brother off the dough.

There was a Stanley-shaped dent in it.

'I'm so sorry, Pete!' said Stanley.

But Pete was staring at the dent with a strange smile on his face.

‘The next big idea!’ Pete said. ‘It’s BIG!’

Pete started racing around the bakery. The boys didn't know exactly what his plan was, but they rushed to help.

Stanley and Arthur helped mix a giant batch of cookie dough.

They rolled it out on the table.

Then Pete pulled up a chair.

'Stanley, would you climb up here and fall on the dough again?'

'OK,' said Stanley. 'But does it have to be face-first this time?' Pete grinned and shook his head.

Stanley got up on the chair. He took a deep breath and fell backwards.

Pete and Arthur carefully cut out the dough around Stanley. Then they pulled and pulled and helped Stanley stand up.

On the table lay a gingerbread boy.
It was four feet tall, about a foot wide
and half an inch thick.

'Just like you,' Arthur told Stanley.
'Only good-looking!'

The cookie looked even better when it was baked and decorated.

‘Wow,’ said Stanley. ‘This might sound weird, but I want to take a bite of my head.’

‘Not now!’ said Pete. ‘We have three dozen Kid-Size Cookies to make!

The next morning was the Food Fair.

The Lambchops walked down Main Street.

‘Look at that!’ said Mr Lambchop

There was a huge crowd outside Pete’s Sweets.

They were waiting to buy Kid-Size Cookies!

But there were two cookies that weren't for sale.

‘These are for you,’ said Pete. ‘Thanks for saving the day!’

'I always knew I had the sweetest boys in the world!' said Mrs Lambchop.

The boys groaned . . .

And took a bite!